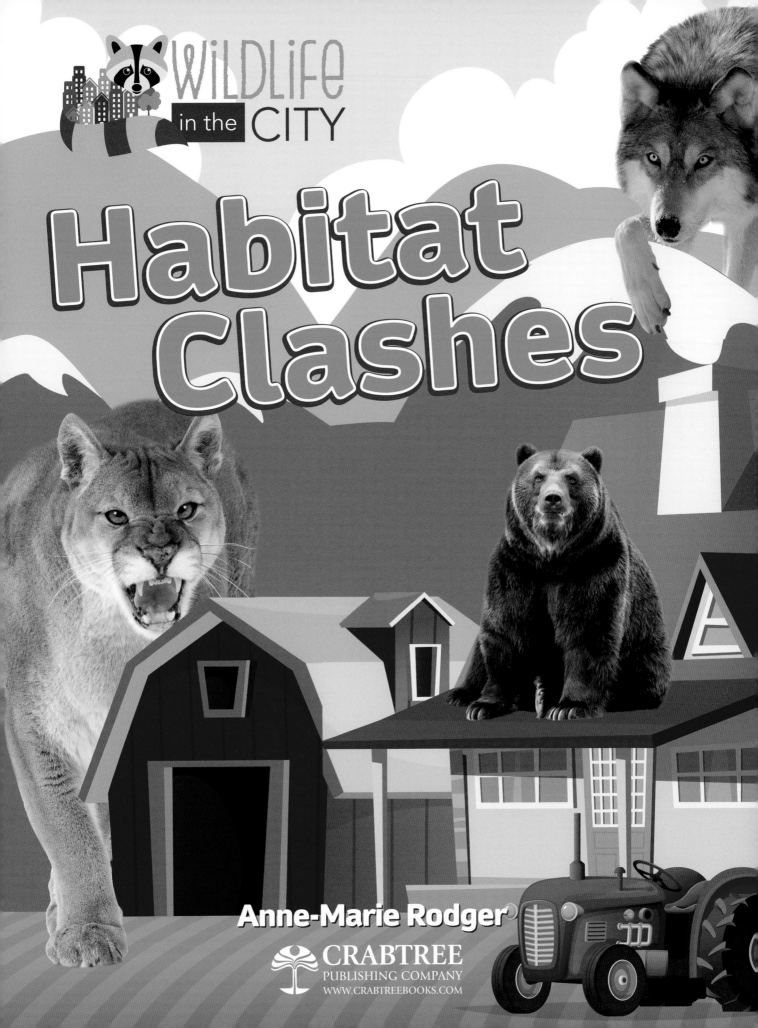

Wildlife
in the CITY

Habitat
Clashes

Anne-Marie Rodger

CRABTREE
PUBLISHING COMPANY
WWW.CRABTREEBOOKS.COM

Author: Anne-Marie Rodger

Editorial director: Kathy Middleton

Art director: Rosie Gowsell Pattison

Editor: Petrice Custance

Proofreader: Wendy Scavuzzo

**Production coordinator and
  Prepress technician:** Ken Wright

Print coordinator: Katherine Berti

Images

Getty Images: Nick Garbutt /
Barcroft Media: p28

All other images
from Shutterstock

Produced for Crabtree Publishing by
Plan B Book Packagers
www.planbbookpackagers.com

Library and Archives Canada Cataloguing in Publication

Title: Habitat clashes / Anne-Marie Rodger.
Names: Rodger, Anne-Marie, author.
Description: Series statement: Wildlife in the city | Includes index.
Identifiers: Canadiana (print) 20190128348 |
  Canadiana (ebook) 20190128356 |
  ISBN 9780778766896 (hardcover) |
  ISBN 9780778767053 (softcover) |
  ISBN 9781427124166 (HTML)
Subjects: LCSH: Urban animals—Juvenile literature. | LCSH: Wildlife
  pests—Juvenile literature. | LCSH: Urban ecology (Sociology)—Juvenile
  literature. | LCSH: Human-animal relationships. | LCSH: Nature—Effect of
  human beings on—Juvenile literature.
Classification: LCC QH541.5.C6 R62 2019 | DDC j591.75/6—dc23

Library of Congress Cataloging-in-Publication Data

Names: Rodger, Anne-Marie, author.
Title: Habitat clashes / Anne-Marie Rodger.
Description: New York, New York : Crabtree Publishing Company, [2020] |
  Series: Wildlife in the city | Includes index.
Identifiers: LCCN 2019029583 (print) | LCCN 2019029584 (ebook) |
  ISBN 9780778766896 (hardcover) |
  ISBN 9780778767053 (paperback) |
  ISBN 9781427124166 (ebook)
Subjects: LCSH: Animals--Adaptation--Juvenile literature. | Habitat
  (Ecology)--Modification--Juvenile literature. | Animals--Food--Juvenile
  literature.
Classification: LCC QH541.14 .R63 2020 (print) | LCC QH541.14 (ebook)
  | DDC 577--dc23
LC record available at https://lccn.loc.gov/2019029583
LC ebook record available at https://lccn.loc.gov/2019029584

Crabtree Publishing Company
www.crabtreebooks.com   1-800-387-7650

Printed in the U.S.A./102019/CG20190809

Published in Canada
Crabtree Publishing
616 Welland Ave.
St. Catharines, Ontario
L2M 5V6

Published in the United States
Crabtree Publishing
PMB 59051
350 Fifth Avenue, 59th Floor
New York, New York 10118

Published in the United Kingdom
Crabtree Publishing
Maritime House
Basin Road North, Hove
BN41 1WR

Published in Australia
Crabtree Publishing
Unit 3–5 Currumbin Court
Capalaba
QLD 4157

CONTENTS

TERRITORY TROUBLES

Got a bear in your backyard? How about a wolf in your pasture? As cities and towns gobble up more land for **subdivisions** and malls, they pave over animal **habitat**. At the same time, pipelines are built smack-dab through animal **migration** routes. **Climate change** has also brought more droughts, fires, and floods that threaten wild areas. Is it any wonder that wild animals are competing with humans for territory?

Throughout the world, humans and human industry now share more territory with truly wild animals than ever before.

CLASH OF THE TITANS

The wild animals people now see more often in the areas we call home are called "human avoiders." These animals normally shy away from, or avoid, humans. They include mountain lions, gray wolves, gray foxes, and bears. Avoiders survive better when humans are not around. When they become too used to living near humans, they eat our garbage or **prey on** farm animals and pets. This leads to clashes between the interests of humans and wild animals.

WWF

World Wildlife Fund (WWF) is the world's largest **conservation** organization. Formed in 1961, it tries to reduce the impact humans have on the environment. WWF operates in more than 100 countries. One of its goals is to encourage people to help preserve habitats. In 2018, WWF got 119 businesses to sign an agreement to stop forest removal from the Brazilian Cerrado. The Cerrado is a **tropical savanna** that is home to thousands of rare plants and animals. It was being cleared for farms and cattle grazing—pushing out animals such as ocelots, jaguars, and cougars.

Wild animals will go for an easy meal if one is offered in backyards and garbage dumps.

HOME HABITAT

People sometimes move to the country to get away from busy cities. Others live in subdivisions built on formerly **rural** lands. These areas are also the home of wild animals.

Mountain lions are fast. They can also climb 12 foot (3.6 m) fences and leap 15 feet (4.6 m) up into a tree.

Backyard bird feeders in some areas attract animals such as elk which in turn attract bears. Some towns and cities are outlawing the feeders because they can contribute to human-animal clashes.

Gray wolves have made a comeback in California. They had been hunted out of existence in 1924. Then, in 2011, a lone wolf was spotted near Mount Shasta. It was likely from Oregon. Other wolves followed. Now, a "Shasta pack" lives near the mountain.

Gray foxes dine on crops such as corn and apples in rural areas in the summer and fall. They live in forests and on the outskirts of cities.

Most wolves fear people and avoid them. Some will prey on domesticated **animals such as cattle or sheep ranches for food.**

Black bears are attracted to garbage dumps located on the outskirts of some cities. They dig through garbage for food.

HUMANS IN THE NEIGHBORHOOD

Some animals mark trees and bushes in their territory with their scent. Songbirds establish their territory by singing. Humans clear land for their farms, ranches, factories, and homes. We often think that only wild animals defend their territory against intruders. But people do it, too. When our population expands, the natural habitat around us shrinks. This becomes a problem when we battle wild animals over space and food.

HUMAN-WILDLIFE CONFLICT

In some rural areas, ranchers and farmers must keep a watchful eye on their **livestock**. Wolves and mountain lions are prey animals. If there is easy access, some will make a meal out of cattle or sheep. When wolves eat too many, ranchers try to protect their herds. Culls, or controlled killings, are a **controversial** way to prevent wild animals from killing livestock. Farmers, ranchers, and businesses believe it is sometimes necessary. Animal conservationists believe culling is cruel and there are other ways to protect livestock.

Aldo Leopold Foundation

Aldo Leopold was an American conservationist who believed people should have a caring relationship with nature and wild animals. He called this relationship a "land ethic." Leopold had once worked for the U.S. Forestry Service. He killed wolves, bears, and mountain lions that threatened ranchers' animals in New Mexico. This experience made him believe humans had a responsibility to care for the land and all animals. He went on to write and teach about this until his death in 1948. Today, the Aldo Leopold Foundation in Baraboo, Wisconsin carries on his conservation work and helps train new conservationists.

Some ranchers put donkeys with their sheep to protect against predators.

Forestry and pipeline building can disrupt animal habitats. This forces wild animals into different areas, including nearby towns and cities.

GATOR AT THE POOL!

American alligators were once an endangered species in the United States. They were protected from hunting in 1967. These clever reptiles made a huge comeback—in neighborhoods as well as the rivers, lakes, swamps, and marshes of Florida and Louisiana. Now they are thriving.

Baby alligators measure 6 to 8 inches (15-20 cm) long and are identified by their long yellow and black stripes.

Humans moved into alligator territory when there weren't many left. Now that alligator numbers have increased, you can find them living on or near golf courses and in human-made ponds and canals. Some occasionally end up in backyard pools!

The average adult male alligator is 10 to 15 feet (3-5 m) long. Its powerful tail makes up half of its length.

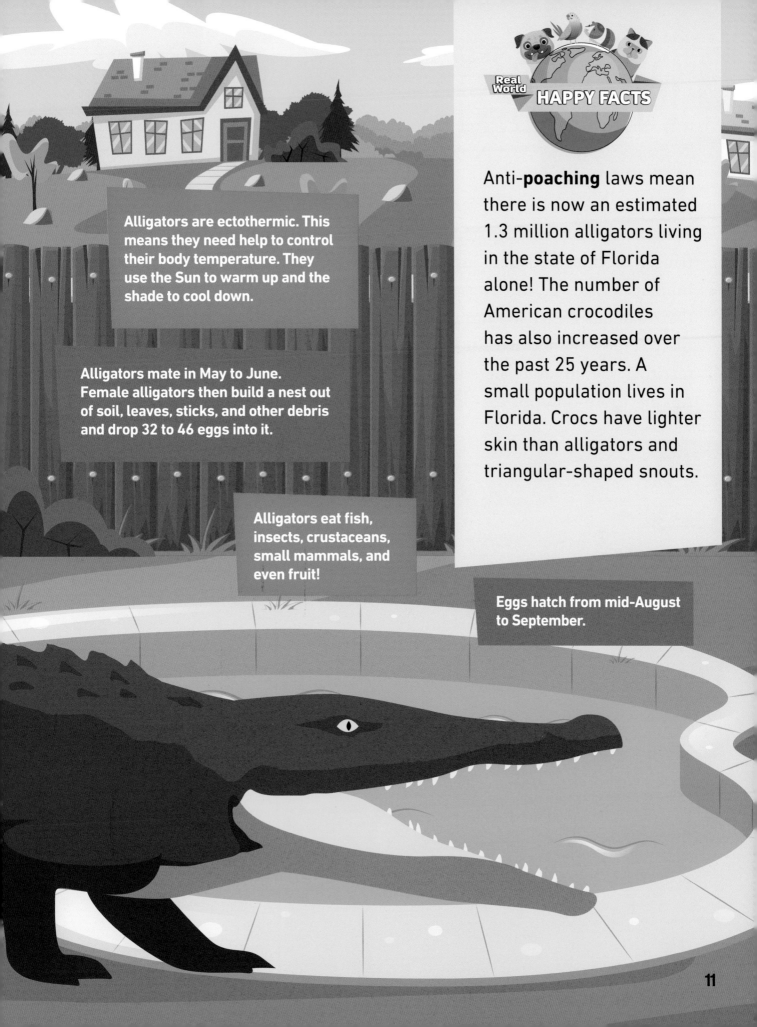

Alligators are ectothermic. This means they need help to control their body temperature. They use the Sun to warm up and the shade to cool down.

Alligators mate in May to June. Female alligators then build a nest out of soil, leaves, sticks, and other debris and drop 32 to 46 eggs into it.

Alligators eat fish, insects, crustaceans, small mammals, and even fruit!

Anti-**poaching** laws mean there is now an estimated 1.3 million alligators living in the state of Florida alone! The number of American crocodiles has also increased over the past 25 years. A small population lives in Florida. Crocs have lighter skin than alligators and triangular-shaped snouts.

Eggs hatch from mid-August to September.

WILD CATS

Wild cats are native to several areas of the United States and Canada. They generally keep to forests and fringes of cities and rural areas. They like to stay clear of humans. However, their territory is being taken over and their habitats are changing. There are many pressures on them. Freeways and **urban sprawl** run through their territories. Climate change is causing more wildfires, forcing these outdoor cats into new areas.

There are fewer than 100 Florida panthers living wild in south Florida. They were nearly hunted to extinction until the 1950s. Today, they are threatened by housing development and vehicles on highways.

WARNING

MOUNTAIN LION COUNTRY A RISK

MOUNTAIN LIONS MAY BE PRESENT AND ARE UNPREDICTABLE. BE CAUTIOUS. THEY HAVE BEEN KNOWN TO ATTACK WITHOUT WARNING. YOUR SAFETY CANNOT BE GUARANTEED. YOU ARE ADVISED TO STAY ALERT TO POTENTIAL DANGERS.

REPORT ALL MOUNTAIN LION SIGHTINGS TO THE PARK OFFICE.

Mountain lions near the coast of British Columbia, Canada eat deer, harbor seals, and sea lions. But raccoons are their top source of food.

CAT THREATS

Wild cat habitat is fragmented, meaning that it exists in pieces between forests, human homes, and highways. Habitat fragmentation makes it difficult for animals to travel their full **range** without being run over by cars. It also means some cats don't travel as far to breed. **Interbreeding** creates populations that are less healthy. In the U.S., Canada lynxes are threatened by forest and timber removal, as well as trapping. Their population is not under threat in Canada. Ocelots used to range from Texas through Arkansas, and Louisiana. Today, only 50 of these spotted cats survive in the U.S. They are threatened by farm and highway expansions. A border wall with Mexico will block their breeding territory.

Look Around You

You may have wild cats living near you but not know it. You are more likely to see evidence of their presence, such as poop or paw prints. And that's a good thing. Being wild-cat-aware can save your life. The British Columbia Conservation Foundation has a website at https://wildsafebc.com that promotes conservation and wild animal safety. California's Department of Fish and Wildlife has a "Keep Me Wild" Campaign that gives advice on how to be aware of wild animals, including cougars. To prevent interactions, CDFW advises people in cat country to keep pets and livestock safe, secure garbage, and eliminate food sources such as pet or animal food.

COUGAR TOWN

In some areas of the U.S. and Canada, it really is a jungle out there. But the jungle is shrinking. Mountain lions once roamed from the east to west coast of North America. Humans gradually took over their territory in the east. Now their habitat in the U.S. and Canada is mostly in the west.

Los Angeles, California is home to many mountain lions. They mostly live in the hills and mountains surrounding the city.

They are predators that hunt on their own. Their prey depends on where they live. In California, they eat mule deer, other deer, elk, raccoons, and even seals. Florida panthers eat feral hogs and armadillos.

Females have a litter of cubs ever two to three years. Litters can range from one to six cubs.

Mountain lions are one of the largest cat species. Adult males weigh 117 to 220 pounds (53-100 kg) and measure 8 feet (2.5 m).

The largest wildlife crossing in the U.S. is being built across the Ventura Freeway (Route 101) in southern California. It will connect the Simi Hills and Santa Susana Mountains with the Santa Monica Mountains. The crossing will prevent mountain lions from being hit by cars when they travel to different areas of their range.

These cats growl, chirp, and hiss, but do not roar.

In areas where they overlap human territory, cougars have occasionally attacked humans. They mostly come into conflict when they threaten domestic animals and livestock.

Mountain lions are known by many names including cougars, pumas, panthers, catamounts, shadow cats, and even ghost cats.

THE BEAR FACTS

Bears are beloved animals, especially in books, movies, and as mascots. That's not always the case when bear country means your backyard. These shaggy mammals sometimes come into conflict with humans.

American black bears are a common sight in some garbage dumps in Canada and the U.S. Some are considered "nuisance bears" because they hang around human settlements too much.

BEAR BUFFET

Housing, ranches, and farms are **intruding** on bear territory. Often, bears will move through a community to get to a natural food source such as a stream where they can grab fish. Problems arise when they stick around and start **foraging** in garbage and eating human food. They become what bear scientists call "food-conditioned." Bears are naturally wary of humans. Food-conditioned bears can lose that wariness and allow humans to get too close. This is dangerous for both the humans and the bears. If the bears get frightened or territorial, they may charge and harm humans. In some communities, threatening bears are caught and **euthanized**.

Look Around You

If you live in bear country, chances are you are very bear-aware. For everybody else, being bear-aware means learning how wild bears behave in real life. Bears are not like they are portrayed in movies. They might look cute, but they are not cuddly. They are not always aware, but they are curious and often predictable. Spend some time reading about bears and bear behavior (check out the bearsmart.com website). Then read a book or watch a movie that portrays bear behavior. Make a list of how the bears in the book or movie "act." Are they realistic? Does their behavior fit with what we know about real wild bears?

BEARS IN TOWN

After a summer of dining off the land, a male black bear can weigh up to 300 pounds (136 kg). They weigh far less in spring or if they have had a hungry summer where forest fires destroy parts of their habitat. It is not uncommon for bears to wander into cities in their range. Some cities even have "report-a-bear" programs in which residents share information on bear sightings through a website.

They have short, sharply curved claws that help them tear into rotten logs for insects and garbage bags for food waste.

Breeding season is May to July. Cubs are born in dens in January to February. They feed on their mother's milk until spring.

Bears have an incredible sense of smell. If they sniff out and find food around humans or human homes, they will keep coming back.

Bears have few predators in the wild. They can travel hundreds of miles searching for food.

Mother bears are protective and may raise cubs for two or more years.

Despite their name, they can be red, brown, patchy, or even white. White black bears are called kermode bears. They live in British Columbia.

Real World HAPPY FACTS

When hungry or curious, black bears are skilled at breaking into and entering properties. A bear broke into a home in Missoula, Montana through a locked door. It managed to lock itself in and fell asleep in a closet. Police could not coax the bear to leave and had to call in Fish and Wildlife experts to **tranquilize** and remove the bear **squatter**.

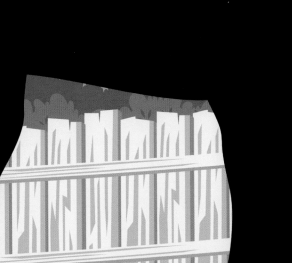

POLAR ROAMERS

Polar bears are Arctic specialists. These big bears are known for their enormous paws, white fur, and giant appetite. Fewer than 25,000 polar bears now live in the wild due to a shrinking sea-ice habitat. Many are now adapting to climate change by spending longer stretches of time near human settlements. Here, they eat human garbage.

Polar bear diets are up to 80 percent meat. Their favorite foods are ringed seals and bearded seals.

Arctic sea ice takes longer to freeze in fall and melts faster in spring. This means more bears search for food in territory that humans also occupy. They find the food at garbage dumps and sometimes by breaking into homes.

Polar bears have no fear of humans. They have been known to attack humans while looking for food.

Real World HAPPY FACTS

Adult male polar bears can weigh from 700 to 1,500 pounds (318–680 kg). Females are half the size of males. Polar bears have 4 inches (10 cm) of fat to insulate their bodies.

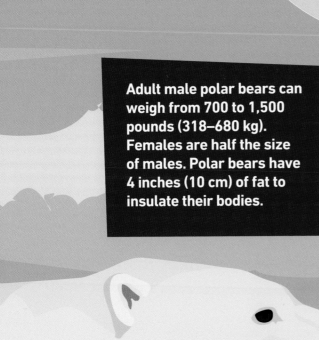

Churchill, Manitoba, Canada is called the polar bear capital of the world. The tiny town on the shores of Hudson Bay gets plenty of tourists. They come to see the bears migrate through each fall. The town also has a polar bear jail where they keep bears who spend too much time scrounging for food in town. These bears are held in concrete cells with bars for at least 30 days. They are fed only snow and water. This is to stop them from thinking that jail and the town are places to get food. They are then released away from town in winter when the ice freezes over and they can hunt for seals.

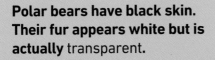

Polar bears have black skin. Their fur appears white but is **actually** transparent.

Polar bears mate from April to June. Females build dens in snow in the winter and have between one and three cubs in December or January. The cubs stay with their mothers for two to three years.

WOLVES AND PEOPLE

Humans have a long history of fearing and hating wolves. Those feelings have usually been based on myths and exaggerated stories of wolves with human-like personalities. When we describe an animal as vicious and cruel, it makes it easier for us to hunt them down and destroy them.

Gray wolves were listed as endangered in the U.S. under the Endangered Species Act (ESA) in 1974.

WOLF CLASHES

Human distrust of wolves comes from wolves doing what they naturally do. They are predators that kill and eat other animals. This can include wild animals such as deer, or livestock such as sheep or cattle. Humans also hunt and raise those animals for food. Centuries of human-wolf clashes led to the near **extinction** of wolves in many areas of the world. The gray wolf was almost wiped out in the United States by 1950. They have made a comeback due to conservation programs.

Reintroduced Wolves

Yellowstone Park was the first National Park in the United States. Set up in 1872, it is located on land in the states of Wyoming, Montana, and Idaho. Gray wolves were native to the park, but were wiped out in 1926. They were **reintroduced** to the park in 1995 and thrive there today. But when they leave the park boundaries, they become fair game to hunters and ranchers. Idaho and Montana have wolf-management plans. The plans allow hunting and are intended to reduce livestock conflict.

When wolves are not protected, hunts are allowed. Some allow unlimited killing.

GRAY WOLF

Gray wolves are large and swift, and generally avoid humans. At one time, wolves ranged throughout all of North America. Human settlements and farming pushed them to the margins. Their territories still overlap areas where humans farm and ranch, which leads to conflict.

Adult male wolves can weigh at least 80 pounds (36 kg) with the heaviest recorded being 175 pounds (79.4 kg)

They have a good sense of smell.

Wolves are carnivores, or meat eaters. Their strong jaws and teeth are made for crushing bones.

They defend their territory by scent marking, scratching, and howling.

They have territories that range in size from 14 square miles (36 square km) to 2, 422 square miles (6, 273 square km). Their territory depends on how much prey there is in the area.

In farming and ranching areas, wolves will prey on cattle, sheep, and other farm animals.

Wolves mate in winter and pups are born in spring. Litters are usually between five and six pups.

Some ranchers in wolf country practice predator-friendly ranching. They use fences, lights, guard dogs, donkeys, and horses to protect their livestock. By doing so, they save more of their animals as well as wolves—since hunting is not the main effort used to control losses.

They shed their dense fur coats in the spring. They can be many colors, from black to gray-blond and even white.

Wolves are social animals, meaning they live in family packs of 5 to 11 animals.

Their prey depends on where they live and includes large mammals such as deer and elk, hares, snakes, squirrels, and foxes.

TREE-CLIMBING FOX

What's that rustling in the trees, jumping from branch to branch? Is it a bird gathering twigs for its nest? How about a squirrel collecting seeds and nuts? Nope! It's the gray fox! This small **canid** is from the same family as wolves, coyotes, and domesticated dogs. Its distinguishing feature is its ability to climb trees.

PUSHED OUT

The gray fox was once the most common fox in the eastern U.S. Mass clearing of its forest habitat for cities and farms pushed it out and allowed the red fox to take over. Without forests, this tree climber's numbers shrunk. Red foxes were better at adapting. Gray foxes don't like to live near humans, but they have been forced to share their space. In urban areas, they are more active at night to avoid people. They can be found in forests near farmlands in southern Canada, mountainous areas of the northwest United States, the plains, and into Central America.

Humane Society Wildlife Land Trust

The Humane Society Wildlife Land Trust (HSWLT) is a charity that protects natural habitats. It also works with landowners such as farmers to provide wildlife sanctuaries. These are places and lands where wild animals can live undisturbed by humans. The HSWLT also fights against poaching, or illegal hunting of wild animals. It offers rewards for the arrest and conviction of poachers. The HSWLT estimates only one to five percent of poachers are caught. Many poachers kill for sport. The HSWLT's anti-poaching rewards campaign gets ordinary citizens involved in stopping the illegal killing of wild animals in North America.

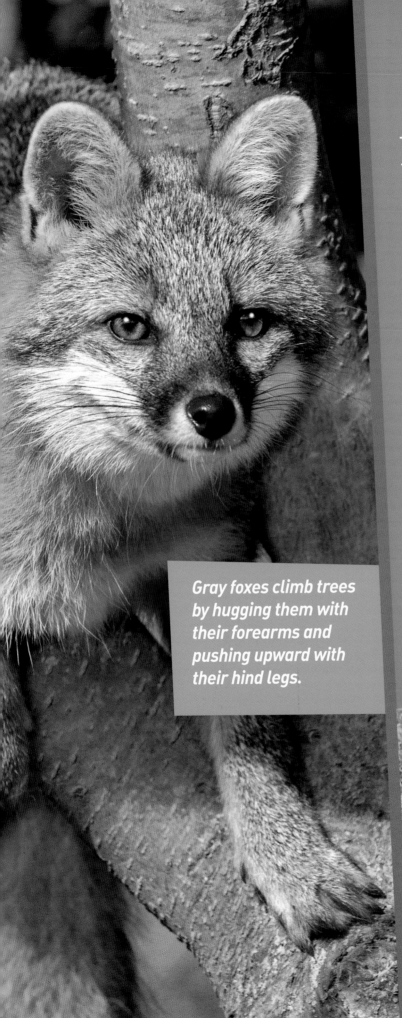

Gray foxes climb trees by hugging them with their forearms and pushing upward with their hind legs.

ELEPHANTS IN THE VILLAGE

Every November, a small herd of elephants walks through a hotel lodge in the African country of Zambia. Each day for five or six weeks, they head to the lodge's garden to eat wild mangoes. Then they head back out. No one stops them. The lodge was built on the herd's traditional territory in South Luangwa National Park.

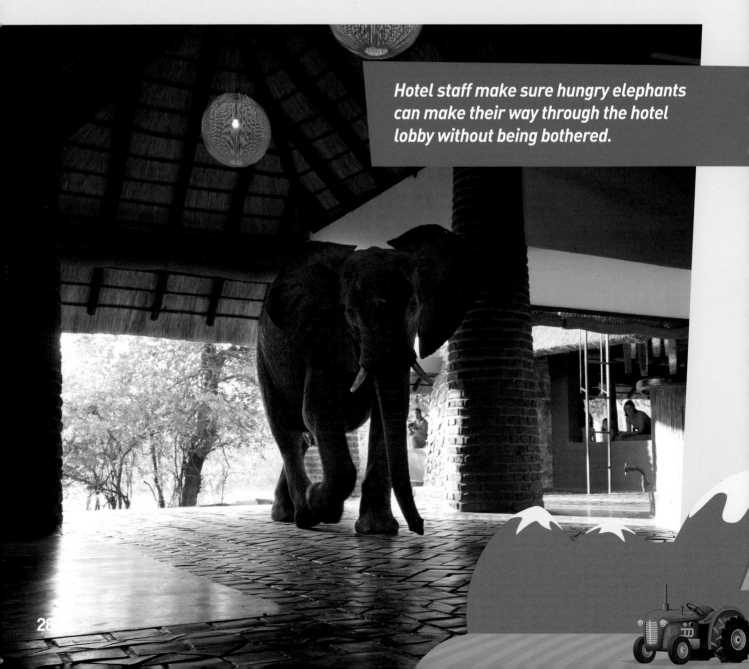

Hotel staff make sure hungry elephants can make their way through the hotel lobby without being bothered.

ELEPHANT CLASHES

The South Luangwa herd's relationship with the lodge is unusual. Guests aren't allowed to get near the elephants and the lodge has not tried to stop the mango raids. The park also protects the herd. More often, people clash with elephants over land, water, and food. Many elephants live close to settled areas in Africa and Asia. To protect crops from elephant raiders in countries throughout Africa, some farmers and communities have built electric fences. The fences work but critics say they interrupt elephant migrations. Poorer farmers also can't afford fences. Conservationists have suggested other methods to prevent human–elephant clashes.

Coexistence as Sweet as Honey

To protect their crops, farmers in Africa sometimes call game officers to shoot and kill raiding elephants. To cut down on raids and save elephants, researchers from University of the Free State in South Africa worked with farmers in southern Tanzania on elephant-proofing solutions. They adopted a conservation program that was first pioneered in Kenya. Farmers and researchers attached beehives to wire fences. When the elephants tried to cross the fences, they were disturbed by angry bees. The beehive didn't eliminate elephant raids entirely, but it reduced them. Farmers also made fewer calls to shoot elephants and were able to **harvest** honey, as well!

Farmers also tried tying cloths soaked in chili-infused oil to rope fences. Heavy rains made that solution difficult to reapply.

LEARNING MORE

Books

Daniels, Patricia. *Ultimate Explorer Field Guide: Mammals.* National Geographic Kids, 2019.

Jazynka, Kitson. *Mission: Wolf Rescue.* National Geographic Kids, 2014.

O'Brien, Cynthia. *Bringing Back the Gray Wolf.* Crabtree Publishing, 2019.

Pallotta, Jerry. *Who Would Win? Polar Bear vs. Grizzly Bear.* Scholastic, 2015.

Websites

www.nwf.org/Educational-Resources/Wildlife-Guide/Mammals/Polar-Bear
Learn fun facts and lots of interesting information about polar bears.

www.earthrangers.com/wildwire/gray-foxes/
Earth Rangers works with Nature Conservancy of Canada to promote a Bring Back the Wild campaign for gray foxes.

www.dec.ny.gov/education/40248.html
Conservationist for Kids magazine is free to fourth grade classes in New York State. Ask an adult to help you download the file.

www.bearsmart.com
This website offers a lot of information on bear behavior and how to live safely around bears.

GLOSSARY

canid A mammal of the dog family

climate change A change in global or regional climate patterns caused by increased levels of carbon dioxide in Earth's atmosphere

conservation The act of preserving or protecting wildlife

controversial Causing public disagreement

domesticated Describing animals that are tame or that live closely with humans

euthanized Put an animal to death humanely, or without causing pain

extinction When all members of a species have died out

feral An escaped or abandoned animal that has become wild

foraging Searching for food

habitat The natural environment of a living thing

harvest To gather for food

interbreeding Animals breeding with other species, such as dogs with wolves

intruding Going into a space where one is not welcome, or altering an environment

livestock Farm animals

migration Moving from one habitat or region to another

poaching Illegal hunting

predators Animals that kill and eat other animals for food

prey on Hunt and kill for food

range The area an animal lives in

reintroduced Brought an animal back to an area where it used to live

rural Of or about the countryside

squatter Someone or something that occupies land or a building that is not theirs

subdivisions Areas of land in cities where homes are built

tranquilize Using drugs to temporarily calm an animal or make it sleep

transparent See-through or clear

tropical savanna Wooded grassland

urban sprawl City expansion

INDEX

QUESTIONS & ANSWERS

Q: How can I help wild animals that share human territory?

A: The first thing you can do is educate yourself. Wild animals do not just live in unpopulated areas of the world. Ask your parents or teachers to help you find information on the animals that share your environment. Learn about the wildlife that live near you.

Q: What should I do if I see a bear in my neighborhood?

A: Bears usually avoid people but if you see one, you should remain calm and stop what you are doing. If the bear is unaware of you, try to move away from it quietly. If it is aware of you, speak calmly to let the bear know you are human and not prey. Back slowly away from the bear's path.